SIGIL™

Mark of Power

D0963375

Chapter 1

1.5

2

3

4

5

6

7

CREATORS

Barbara Kesel
Writer

Ben Lai
Penciler

Ray Lai
Inker

Wil Quintana
Colorist

Dave Lanphear
Letterer

SIGIL #6

Steve McNiven
Penciler

Jordi Ensign
with Batt
Inkers

JD Smith
Colorist

SIGIL #5 Ink Assist

Don Hillsman II

SIGIL #6 cover:
Steve McNiven
Penciler
Ray Lai
Inker
Wil Quintana
Colorist

SIGIL #7

Kevin Sharpe
Penciler

Randy Elliott
Inker

Wil Quintana
Colorist

SIGIL #7 cover:
Kevin Sharpe
Penciler
Don Hillsman II
Inker
Wil Quintana
Colorist

CROSSGEN CHRONICLES #1

Ron Marz
with Barbara Kesel
Writers

Claudio Castellini
Penciler

Caesar Rodriguez
with Andrew Crossley
CG Inkers

Michael Atiyeh
Colorist

The CrossGen Universe created by Mark Alessi & Gina M. Villa

TRADE PAPERBACK

Cover Painted by Christopher Moeller

DESIGN

Pam Davies
Dave Lanphear
Brandon Peterson
Sylvia Bretz
Troy Peteri

EDITORIAL

Tony Panaccio
Ian M. Feller
Michael A. Beattie
Barbara Kesel
Mark Waid
Gina M. Villa

FOREWORD

"John F. Kennedy, when asked how he had become a war hero, replied, 'It was involuntary. They sank my boat.'"
Quoted by
Arthur M. Schlesinger, Jr.,
author of *A Thousand Days*

What makes a hero? Now, that's a very loaded question, with about as many answers as there are stars in the sky. So let's narrow it down. When I think of heroes, I think of people who, regardless of their abilities or preparedness, place someone else's needs before their own and then make a sacrifice in order to help someone. Granted, that's a very broad definition, but that's what I think.

So what makes a person sacrifice something for someone else? At what point in time does his psychological makeup — which is shaped by his upbringing, his life experience and his philosophies — match up with a mission or a cause and turn his motives from selfish to selfless?

This isn't a rhetorical question asked so I can spout out my philosophies on heroes and villains. I change my own answers pretty regularly. No, I asked because I was actually counting on Samandahl Rey to tell me.

We created Sam, and the whole cast of characters in *Sigil*, to explore that very basic theme of the reluctant hero. In fact, before we came up with the final title of *Sigil*, we used the working title "The Unwilling Hero" in all of our brainstorming meetings.

You see, Sam isn't a hero. Not yet, at least. And he isn't sure he knows how to be one. That's what we thought would be an interesting story to tell. In most hero-oriented comic books, the "origin" story is the big key. Take an inherently good character, slap him down with a tragedy or other life-changing event, provide him a power and/or a costume, and by the end of issue #1, you've got instant hero.

With Sam, we wanted to make his journey of *becoming* a hero the primary story, not the quest for some powers and a costume. In our stories, the granting of the Sigil, a talisman of unique and unmeasured power in the CrossGen Universe, is not the culmination of a character's "coming of age." It's rarely even a gift in the traditional sense, since at least at first it tends to actually cause more problems than it solves. While it brings certain physical gifts to its bearer, they're accompanied by unexpected and lugubrious burdens. Power can have a corrupting influence on the person who wields it, but it can also have a corrupting influence on the people around it. As you read this volume, you'll see the advantages, the frustrations and the consequences inherent in the manifestation of instant power, and the beginning of how

Sam comes to deal with power first as a man, and second, as a hero-to-be.

Of course, you'll also get one heck of a science fiction story, to boot. Now, at this point, I want people to take notice that we haven't used the term "science fiction" until now. Yes, *Sigil* is a story set in a world populated by a wide variety of science fiction conventions – aliens, spaceships, ray guns, and stuff like that – but it's not a "science fiction story." It's a hero's story set against a science fiction backdrop, but Sam's character is universal. He could be Rick in *Casablanca* (which *Sigil* writer Barbara Kesel will tell you later in this volume was a great inspiration for her in writing these first seven issues), he could be Nick Nolte in a "buddy cop" movie, or Clint Eastwood in any number of his early westerns. To propel Sam on his quest, we could have put him anywhere, in any time, to tell the story. So why science fiction?

Well, blame Patrick Stewart and Gene Roddenberry. Yes, I am a fan of *Star Trek: The Next Generation*, which is still, to date, the best-executed vision of what that franchise was meant to be. Patrick Stewart's performances as Captain Jean Luc Picard represent, in many ways, the complete antithesis to the man that Sam Rey is at the beginning of *Sigil*. Where Picard is a thinking man's hero who analyzes each crisis and finds answers through the strength of his experience and wisdom, Sam's

solution to most problems is to destroy things. And that's what will make Sam's voyage dynamic and interesting. Deep down, he wants to be that wiser, more thoughtful hero, but he is constantly struggling against his natural tendency to be more combative than constructive. Who knows which way he'll gravitate? Against the backdrop of the classic space opera, the possibilities are limitless. Space provides a grand scale and an unlimited template for action and adventure, giving *Sigil* a great launching pad for a story that has the potential to be dynamically unlike any other space opera ever told before – because, in this science fiction setting, there is one x-factor that doesn't exist anywhere else – the unpredictability of the CrossGen Universe. Sigils and god-like beings intermix with SF concepts and ideas to form a backdrop on a grand mythological scale. We're able to bring you a world where you really don't know what is going to, or for that matter, *could* happen next.

So, as you're reading this volume, remember I'll be reading right along with you, searching for the answers between the captions and the splash pages, looking for the hero that resides in each of us. ↻

MARK

Mark Alessi

This place grows colder, my friend. Its energy wanes. I am seeking a solution, and eagerly welcome your thoughts.

It is not like you to be so troubled.

So long ago, when it was all set in motion, it was so... fascinating in its complexity. It surprised even me. Now things are static, worlds grow cold, and what were once glorious fields of battle lay still and barren.

The problem is not simply lazy warriors. The vital energies on which we all depend are fading away... it shouldn't happen like this... yet it is! It is dying, and the first do nothing to prevent it!

Because the first don't understand. They have no idea of the connection between their actions and the Whole.

Yes. They need...motivation. They must be forced to reignite the cycle...

Yet...they know nothing of my existence. To do so would *change* them...

Chapter 1

Why look only to the first?

THERE ARE MANY WORLDS OPEN TO YOU, SO MANY PEOPLE...

IF YOU WERE TO STEP IN QUIETLY -- WALK AMONG THEM. THEN A SUBTLE TOUCH, TO ADD JUST A SMALL MARK OF YOUR PASSAGE -- A SIGN.

YOUR SIGN.

IMAGINE... EACH WORLD, ONE SOUL, MARKED WITH THE SIGIL. OPENED TO THE POWER.

Why just one?

I WAS THINKING IN TERMS OF EFFICIENCY. THE NUMBER IS UNIMPORTANT. A SMALL NUMBER MAKES FOR A CLEAR BURDEN ON EACH; TOO MANY, AND THEY LET SOMEONE ELSE DO THE WORK.

AS WE HAVE ALREADY SEEN WITH THE FIRST. STILL...

COME...

HERE... A WORLD WITH UNTAPPED POTENTIAL EAGERLY AWAITING A FOCUS.

A shame that no one here has touched the nature of the mysteries of the Whole before now. The lives of these people must be so very plain.

THEY'RE ON THE EDGES OF AN INTERSTELLAR WAR. I DON'T THINK THEY HAVE THE LEISURE TO PROPERLY APPRECIATE THEIR BOREDOM.

AT LEAST THEY UNDERSTAND THE NATURE OF CONFLICT. THAT'S HALF THE BATTLE.

HMMMM...AND CONFLICT FORMS LEADERS...

I HAVE A FEELING ABOUT THIS PLACE.

WHAT WILL I TELL THEM, THESE... SIGIL-BEARERS?

GIVE THEM NO WARNING, NO DIRECTION; LET THEIR ACTIONS DICTATE THE FLARE OF THE SIGIL.

THIS WILL REENERGIZE YOUR WARRIORS. BRING THEM BACK TO THEIR PURPOSE. HAVE THEM FIGHT OFF THE CHILL OF THEIR CURRENT ENNUI.

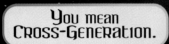

You mean CROSS-GENERATION.

YES, POWER FROM CONFLICT. ENERGY CREATING ENERGY.

AS THE NEW ONES WORK TOWARD THEIR OWN DEFINITION, THEY SERVE YOUR NEEDS.

I TELL YOU, YOU COULD START A NEW CHAIN OF CREATION TO STOKE THE COOLING FIRES OF THE WHOLE.

I FEEL IT GROWING WARMER ALREADY.

SO WE'VE GOT ENOUGH TO LAST THE WEEK, BUT IF NO WORK SHOWS UP BY THEN...

...I'LL JUST SELL MYSELF TO THE SULTAN AND YOU CAN LIVE OFF THE PROCEEDS.

SOUNDS LIKE A PLAN TO ME.

YEAH?

I HEAR YOU'RE LOOKING FOR SOME TOOTH'N' CLAW...

WELL, FRIEND, FOR ONLY THIRTY G-CREDS, I CAN LEAD YOU TO SOME OF THE FINEST PSEUDOSAUR ACTION AVAILABLE ANYWHERE. JUST FOLLOW ME.

OH, NO.

SAM -- AREN'T WE TRYING TO KEEP THINGS UNCOMPLICATED?

SURE. STARTING TOMORROW.

HERE WE GO AGAIN...

STAY IN YOUR PODS -- NO OPERATORS INSIDE THE ARENA AT ANY TIME.

IF WE GET RAIDED, PODS AND EXITS OPEN AUTOMATICALLY. WE DON'T POST BAIL, SO DON'T GET CAUGHT.

PSEUDOSAURS ARE NOT TOYS!

YOU'RE *KILLING* THEM!

MOVE IT, BUDDY. NO SAURIANS IN HERE.

AT THE SIGNAL, ENTER RAPPORT WITH YOUR 'SAUR.

THIS IS POD SIX, *READY.*

GOTCHA, POD SIX. TO CONTINUE: THE POD CONTROLS PUT YOU IN COMMAND OF YOUR PSEUDOSAUR'S MOVEMENTS, SPEED, AND LEVEL OF FEROCITY.

VREEEEEET

ONCE COMBAT BEGINS, THE MATCH CONTINUES UNTIL ONLY ONE 'SAUR IS LEFT MOVING.

THE WINNER MUST SURVIVE COMBAT OR THE HOUSE TAKES THE STAKE.

READY...?

GO!

GRAWWR

DO YOU COME TO THIS BLOODBATH OFTEN?

THIS ISN'T *MY* IDEA OF FUN. I'M JUST HERE WITH MY FRIEND.

FRIEND? NO PREFIX ON THAT?

DEPENDS ON WHO'S ASKING...

"...THERE'S A LOT OF PREDATORS OUT THERE."

NOT ME. I PREFER A GENTLER KIND OF GAME.

WHICH NATURALLY LED YOU TO THE PSEUDOSAUR PIT.

YOU TWO **MIND?**

GRAWWRF

I'M TRYING TO **CONCENTRATE!**

GRAWWWR

LADIES AND GENTLEMEN, WE'RE DOWN TO A CLASSIC TRIANGLE.

TWO GUYS AND ONE LADY LEFT--

WE ALL KNOW **THAT'S** GONNA END IN A FIGHT.

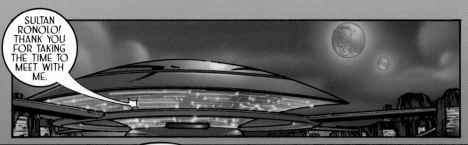

SULTAN RONOLO! THANK YOU FOR TAKING THE TIME TO MEET WITH ME.

YOU KNOW I ALWAYS ENJOY OUR TALKS, MIKEL -- EVEN IF YOU ONLY SUFFER MY PRESENCE IN HOPES THAT *THIS* TIME I WILL FINALLY SET MY SEAL TO THE VESPER ACCORD...

...OR IS IT JUST THAT YOU ENJOY THE VIEW FROM MY PRIVATE LANAI?

BOTH, ACTUALLY. YOUR WIVES ARE BEAUTIFUL AND THE PLANETARY UNION *REALLY* WANTS THAT ACCORD.

OKAY, HERE'S THE SPIEL:

DON'T FORGET THAT IT WAS THE UNION THAT GRANTED YOUR PREDECESSOR THIS WAYSTATION WITH THE UNDERSTANDING THAT TANIPAL WOULD CONTINUE TO ALLY ITSELF WITH THE FIVE WORLDS OF THE UNION.

IT'S TIME TO RENEW, YOU'VE LET IT LAPSE, AND NOW YOU'RE PLAYING US AGAINST THE SAURS.

FOR HOW LONG?

THE SAURIAN FORCES ARE MASSING JUST SHORT OF TANAPALI SPACE.

IF YOU SIGN, YOU'VE GOT OUR PROTEC--

YOU'RE NOT LISTENING TO A WORD I'M SAYING, ARE YOU?

JUST A MOMENT, MIKEL.

TEO, ATTEND ME.

GO SEE WHAT'S WRONG...

SO WHERE'S YOUR NEW FRIEND?

WE'RE MEETING LATER.

WELL, YOU WILL NOT BELIEVE THE WOMAN I JUST SAW. SHE'S--

SHE'S FOR *SALE,* SAM.

HEADS UP. SULTAN'S GUARDS.

WE'RE BUSTED.

ATTENTION! THIS IS NOT A RAID!

I REPEAT: THIS IS NOT A RAID! THIS IS ONLY AN INTERROGATION!

WE WILL BE PASSING AMONG YOU WITH A HOLO.

ONE OF THE SULTAN RONOLO'S WIVES HAS BEEN KIDNAPPED.

ALL SHIPS ARE GROUNDED UNTIL SHE IS SAFELY RECOVERED.

ALL CITIZENS AND VISITORS ARE ADVISED TO JOIN THE SEARCH FOR ZANNIATI.

THIS MIGHT MEAN WORK, SAM. *REAL* WORK. C'MON!

IN A MINUTE. JUST ONE MORE GAME -- MY LUCK'S RUNNING HOT TONIGHT!

"FINE."

TCHLUSARUD HAS DIRECTED ME TO ANSWER ONE QUESTION:

SINCE WE ARE ACTING IN VIOLATION OF TREATY...

...ARE WE CERTAIN THE HUMAN IS INSIDE?

...BUT THEY ALL LOOK ALIKE TO ME.

THIS ONE WAS REPORTED TO BE AN EXACT MATCH TO THE HOLO WE RECEIVED...

NOT THAT I'M COMPLAINING.

SKAPOW

VVHEEEEEN

NOW, I WOULDN'T BE COUNTING ON ENJOYING THAT REWARD, *CORPSE.*

YES. BUT I FIND THAT APPEARANCES ARE OFTEN DECEIVING.

TELL YOU WHAT --

-- IF YOU CAN USE THAT, I CAN GET US OUT OF HERE ALIVE.

TRUST ME.

DO YOU NEED SOME HELP WITH THAT, PRETTY LADY?

DO I *LOOK* LIKE IT?

C'MERE, FELLA!

LET'S CALM YOU DOWN.

I DON'T NEED A ROGUE PSEUDOSAUR WITH A KILL-PAC.

KLIK

THAT'S BETTER, huh?

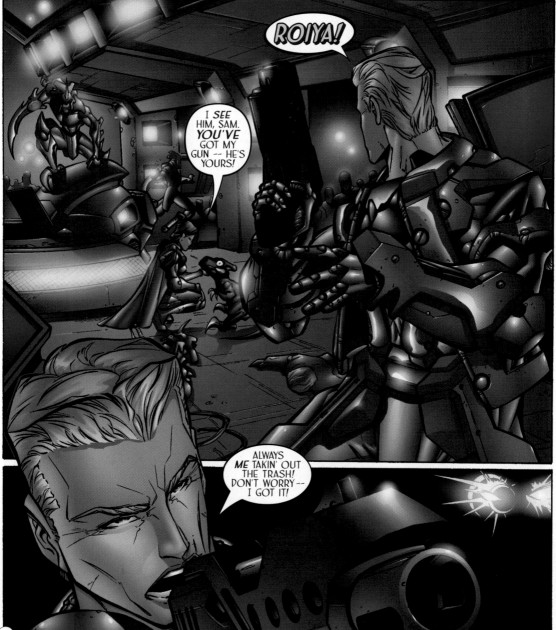

ROIYA!

I *SEE* HIM, SAM. *YOU'VE* GOT MY GUN -- HE'S YOURS!

ALWAYS *ME* TAKIN' OUT THE TRASH! DON'T WORRY -- I GOT IT!

I GO--

OOOOF!

NO! GRAH--UK!

YOU CAN'T--

YOUR EYES...

WHAT THE HELL KIND OF SAURIAN *ARE* YOU?

YOU... YOU WILL FIND THEM, GATHER THEM, AND LEAD THEM.

UNHF!

YOU'RE TOO STRONG FOR NON-COMBATANT CASTE --

ROWA!

TOO LATE, APESPAWN.

YOUR WOMAN IS *MEAT*.

SKREENK

MEAT?

THAT WOULD MAKE *ME* ONE HIGH-CALIBER COW.

TRUST YOU? YOUR PAL TOOK OUT THAT SAUR! YOU'RE GOLDEN.

SHOULDN'T WE GET HER TO AN EMERGENCY MEDIK?

THEY WOULDN'T TAKE HER. WE'RE NOT FROM TANIPAL, WE'RE OFFICIALLY INDIGENT, AND IT HAPPENED IN A NO-LAW ZONE.

YOUR SHIP HAS A MEDIK?

F'COURSE! THOUGH WITH THE HANGARS IN LOCKDOWN...

DON'T WORRY ABOUT THAT. TANIPALI SECURITY.

MY DAY JOB.

ALTHOUGH I'M IN THE PROCESS OF EXECUTING MY SUDDEN RESIGNATION.

HRMMMMMMMMMMMMMMMMMMM

When CrossGen launched in May 2000, the goal was to debut with a splash. An initial release of four monthly titles seemed to be the right number, but asking fans to buy four comics to get a taste of a brand new universe of stories was asking a lot.

Hence, *CrossGen Chronicles* #1 offered an opportunity to sample the characters, worlds and stories surrounding *Mystic, Sigil, Scion* and *Meridian.* The issue featured five-page vignettes respectively showcasing each lead character and storyline. The trick was placing them all within the context of one story, so the choice was made to use the god-like beings of the CrossGen Universe, the First, as a framing device.

It also was decided that the five-page interludes would present the characters just after they'd been granted their sigils, allowing an exploration of how they reacted to those sigils. As far as the timeline was concerned, the sequences would fit between issues #1 and #2 of the individual series. Once the #1 issues hit the stands, perceptive readers would be able to fit together the chronology. Leaving a trail of clues for clever readers to follow would become a CrossGen hallmark.

In *Sigil*, this scene shows Sam in the emotional aftermath of awakening to discover that his best friend is dead. Still in shock from the physical effects of sigil activation and the discovery of two strangers on his ship, the final blow comes when he realizes the ship is speaking to him…in a familiar voice.

Here it is, presented "in sequence" for the first time. ☙

Chapter 1.5

PASSENGERS. OKAY... ...I NEVER GOT *NAMES* OUTTA YOU TWO IN ALL THE EXCITEMENT PLANETSIDE.

JeMERIK MEER. AND SHE'S...

...WELL, SHE'S THE ONE WHO KNEW ENOUGH ABOUT SPACECRAFT TO GET THIS ONE FLYING.

YOU'VE BEEN UNCONSCIOUS EVER SINCE WE LEFT TANIPAL.

I'M GLAD YOU'RE ALL RIGHT...um...

SAM. Uh... YEAH, YOU TOO. WHAT DID YOU SAY YOUR NAME—

HANG ON!

KROOOM

AND WHILE YOU'RE AT IT, TELL ME WHO'S PILOTING THE *BITTERLUCK* NOW.

MEER! WHAT'S GOING ON? WHO'S CHASING US?

LET'S SEE...

THEN SIT YOURSELVES DOWN AND STRAP YOURSELVES IN, IT'S ABOUT TO GET EVEN BUMPIER.

PICKED THE RIGHT *NAME* FOR THIS OLD BUCKET.

WE'VE BEEN DAMN LUCKY SO FAR...

...BECAUSE THERE'S NO WAY THE SHIP'S COMPUTER HAS THE REASONING CAPACITY TO FLY THIS SLICK ON AUTO PILOT.

I DO NOW, SAM.

THAT...

...IT CAN'T BE...

...BUT THAT WAS ROIYA'S VOICE.

Chapter 2

"I wanted Sam to start out on the wrong side of mid-life. When this power comes into his life, it represents the very last chance for him to have an impact on his world."

— *Barbara Kesel*

At CrossGen, we feel that if you're going to borrow a little something, start with the classics.

When we first meet Sam and Roiya, they are having a grand old time on Tanipal, a setting inspired by the classic casino locale of the film *Casablanca*. Tanipal is a planet that exists for pleasure, an intergalactic Las Vegas wedged smack in the middle of an age-old war zone. But no fighting ever takes place there. It's the unspoken "neutral zone" whose sanctity is broken in our first chapter by a brutal surprise invasion of Saurian soldiers.

While Sam and Roiya aren't exactly Humphrey Bogart and Lauren Bacall, *Sigil* writer Barbara Kesel gave their relationship a similar star-crossed quality, mixing Bogie's scoundrel with Bacall's tough exterior.

"*Sigil* is the concept I carried with me driving cross-country when I first moved to Florida from Oregon to take the job as head writer for CrossGen, developing characters and story ideas along the way," Barbara said. "We knew this character, who picked up the name Samandahl Rey somewhere between Iowa and Kentucky, would play a key role in the mythology of the Sigil-Bearers. His code title was 'The Unwilling Hero,' so we always knew that this was not the guy who would be Mr. Stand-Up-And-Take-Charge-and-Be-a-

Hero right off the bat. He would need some simmer time on that burner."

Barbara said she envisioned Sam as a man in his 40s, but "a Harrison Ford forty, 'well-preserved' and still action-hero active.

"I wanted Sam to start out on the wrong side of mid-life," she said. "When this power comes into his life, it represents the very last chance for him to have an impact on his world. He's always been a very good guy on the inside, but the world never rewarded him for that, so he kind of drifted into the ethical twilight zone. Getting the sigil gives him a second chance to be the hero. We wanted someone who was handsome but

---

"Ask Mark Alessi. I'm allergic to doing anything exactly the same way it's been done before."

---

rugged – someone who had some life experience, with more than a few miles on the odometer. We needed a character who had his own preconceived notions, his own prejudices, because our plan was to take all those notions and prove them wrong during the course of the development of his character."

Roiya and Zanniati were characters created to be contrasts, according to Barbara.

"Basically, Roiya's the good girl in the 'tough girl' suit, and Zanni's the tough girl in the 'good girl' suit. Sort of. When we first meet Zanni, she's in the Sultan of Tanipal's harem as his 13th wife, but her outfit does not reflect her true colors."

Needless to say, all of these conventions get turned on their ear when our version of "Rick's Place" (the bar from *Casablanca*, for those of you not familiar with this extraordinary film) is attacked. Roiya, whom many who read comics might assume is a sidekick (because she's female and because she's not the lead character of the comic), is actually the most heroic figure through the first chapter of *Sigil*. While Sam is more of a mercenary scoundrel, *Roiya* is the one who symbolizes heroic sacrifice during Tanipal's invasion, effectively turning yet another science fiction standard on its ear. Her familiar banter with Sam made her seem to some like a love interest – but killing her in the first chapter put a bit of a spoiler on those hopes. So what started out as a nice homage to science fiction and classic film stereotypes ends with just about every preconceived notion turned upside down and inside out.

"Ask Mark Alessi," Barbara joked. "I'm allergic to doing anything exactly the same way it's been done before."

YOU'RE FORGETTING TO FACTOR IN CURRENT EVENTS.

IF TANIPAL WAS COVERED UNDER THE PLANETARY UNION'S VESPER ACCORD, WE'D BE OBLIGATED TO COVER TERRORISM.

BUT IT'S NOT.

THE SULTAN'S KEEPING BOTH SIDES HANGING.

SO WE CALL IT WHAT WE WANT -- HIS CLAIM WILL BE DENIED.

BUT -- CAN YOU SPOT THE *OPPORTUNITY* HERE?

NO, WE NEED A DECLARATION OF WAR TO INSTITUTE DENIAL OF CLAIM ON THAT BASIS. THIS DISASTER APPEARS TO BE THE WORK OF UNLICENSED TECHNOLOGY. NEW WEAPONRY.

SO YOU'RE SAYING IT'S A TERRORIST ACT.

WE FIND EVIDENCE TO LINK THIS INCIDENT TO THE SAURIAN ATTACK...

...THAT SOURS THE SULTAN'S DEALINGS WITH THE SAURIANS.

TANIPAL BECOMES A FORMAL HUMAN ALLY AGAIN.

WE GET A BONUS.

NO SAURIAN DID THIS. BUT TRACKING WHAT DID WILL LIKELY LEAD ME TO MY QUARRY...

"...THE ONE WITH THE SIGIL."

SAM?

YOU GONNA TALK TO ME OR JUST SIT THERE LOOKING STUNNED AND STUPID?

I'M HEARING YOUR VOICE, ROIYA, BUT MY TWO EYES SAW YOUR DEAD BODY-- HOW C'N YOU BE TALKING WITH ME?

I LEFT MY BODY, TRUE, AND I CAN'T GO BACK-- BELIEVE ME, I'VE TRIED.

BUT, SAM, IF THIS IS DEAD... IT'S NOT SO BAD.

PARDON ME FOR NOT VOLUNTEERIN'! BUT HOW--?

DURING THAT EXPLOSION, I FELT MYSELF... GO, BUT SOMETHING CONNECTED ME WITH THE SHIP AND THEN I WAS EVERYWHERE INSIDE OF IT...

WHAT A HORRIBLE EXPERIENCE... TO BE TRAPPED IN DEATH...

BUT SHE'S NOT DEAD. THERE ARE MANY DIFFERENT FORMS OF LIFE...

I SCREWED UP, ROI. I SHOULD HAVE HAD YOUR BACK.

THOSE SAURS--

SNAP OUT OF IT, SOLDIER--

THE SAURIAN SHIPS ARE STRAFING AGAIN.

I NEED YOU IN THE HERE AND NOW.

GOTCHA.

SHOW ME WHAT'S OUT THERE.

GAENA, I HAVE JUST RECEIVED CONFIRMATION THAT THE EXPLOSION FOLLOWING THE SAURIAN ATTACK WAS *NOT* A SAURIAN WEAPON...

...ALTHOUGH THEY CAN'T TELL ME JUST WHAT IT *WAS*.

GREAT. AN UNKNOWN WEAPON THAT GIVES NO WARNING AND LEAVES NO EVIDENCE.

CROSS, DO WE HAVE *ANY* CLUES?

WITNESSES PUT A SMALL SHIP, THE *BITTERLUCK*, AT THE HEART OF THE... ANOMALY.

VINZER?

MY MEN CHECKED OUT PORT RECORDS TO SEE WHO OWNS THE *BITTERLUCK* -- NAME OF ONE SAMANDAHL REY TURNED UP.

HUMAN.

WE HAVE DISPATCHED UNION GUARDS TO BRING HIM IN FOR QUESTIONING. THEY'RE ON AN INTERCEPT AND DETAIN RUN NOW.

THANK YOU, ALAI.

GENTLEMEN, WE REPRESENT THE INTERESTS OF THE FIVE WORLDS HERE ON TANIPAL.

WE ALL KNOW THE STRATEGIC VALUE OF THIS WORLD TO THE PLANETARY UNION. THE SULTAN IS A *VITAL* ALLY.

BUT THIS MYSTERY WEAPON IS *MORE* IMPORTANT.

SO SEND *MORE* GUARDS, SEND *EVERY* AVAILABLE SHIP, *CAPTURE* THE *BITTERLUCK* AND BRING BACK THAT *WEAPON!*

RIGHT NOW, IT'S IN HUMAN HANDS. KEEPING IT IN HUMAN CONTROL COULD CHANGE THE BALANCE OF POWER -- WE'D ALL LIKE THE SAURS AND THE SULTAN TO CATER TO *US*, RIGHT?

DO IT.

IT FOLLOWED US. I THOUGHT IT WAS YOURS.

I *PLAY* THEM, I DON'T PLAY *WITH* THEM!

PLAY NICE, SAM... ...I LIKE HAVING HIM ON BOARD.

HE STAYS!

LOOK: THIS IS WHAT HAPPENED ON TANIPAL.

IT'S A MIRACLE WE SURVIVED.

TANIPALI VIDFEED

RESIDENTIAL BLOCKS

BLAST EPICENTER

GAMING CENTER

WELL *SOME* OF US DID, ANYWAYS...

VERY FUNNY, ROIYA.

BUT WHATEVER KINDA BOMB WENT OFF THERE... THAT'S SOME AMAZING POWER.

THINK THAT'S WHAT GAVE ME THIS MARK?

MORE PROPERLY A SIGIL THAN A MARK.

IT'S NOT JUST RANDOMLY PATTERNED FLESH -- SOMEONE BRANDED YOU.

I RAN A CHECK OF HIS SCANS WHILE YOU WERE SLEEPING IT OFF.

JeMERIK MEER **IS** ONE OF THE SULTAN'S GUARDSMEN... OR WAS.

YOU WERE LEAVING TANIPAL. I HAD TO GET AWAY...

MY HUSBAND IS... A CRUEL MAN. WHEN JeMERIK FOUND ME, I WAS GOING TO COMMANDEER A SHIP TO GO HOME, TO ESCAPE...

INSTEAD I FOUND MYSELF FIGHTING BY YOUR SIDE.

WE... MET. I REMEMBER THAT...

BUT WHY *MY* SHIP?

HE'S ALSO THE GUY WHO WAS MAKING THE MOVES ON ME WHILE YOU WERE PLAYING WITH PSEUDOSAURS...

HE'S NO THREAT, AND NO PROBLEM, AT LEAST NOT WHILE I'M IN THIS FORM...

THE *WOMAN,* ON THE OTHER HAND, DOESN'T EXIST.

I DIDN'T CHOOSE YOUR SHIP...

I CHOSE *YOU.*

WHEN ROIYA WAS... ATTACKED...

I COULDN'T LEAVE YOU. *SOMETHING* MADE ME WANT TO HELP YOU... TO TRUST YOU...

YEAH, SOMETHING. SO -- I GOT ME A DEAD FRIEND, A DRIFTER, A RUNAWAY, AND A BRANDED CHEST.

OKAY, DON'T ANYBODY TALK TO ME.

I GOTTA GO THINK.

IS *THIS*
HOW YOU
ENFORCE OUR
AGREEMENT?

FIRING
ON MY WORLD?
LETTING LOOSE NEW
WEAPONS OF MASS
DESTRUCTION?

JUST THINK
OF THE COST: THE
BUILDINGS *DESTROYED,*
THE LIVES LOST, THE
REVENUES MISSING FROM
THE GAMING CENTERS
THAT NO LONGER
EXIST!

AND
SOMEONE'S
*STOLEN MY
WIFE!*

TANIPAL
HAS HAD A
VERY AGREEABLE
RELATIONSHIP WITH
YOU PEOPLE UNTIL
THIS OUTRAGEOUS
DISPLAY OF
DISRESPECT!

WHAT DO
YOU HAVE TO SAY
FOR YOUR ACTIONS,
TCHLUSARUD?

ARE YOU
FINISHED?

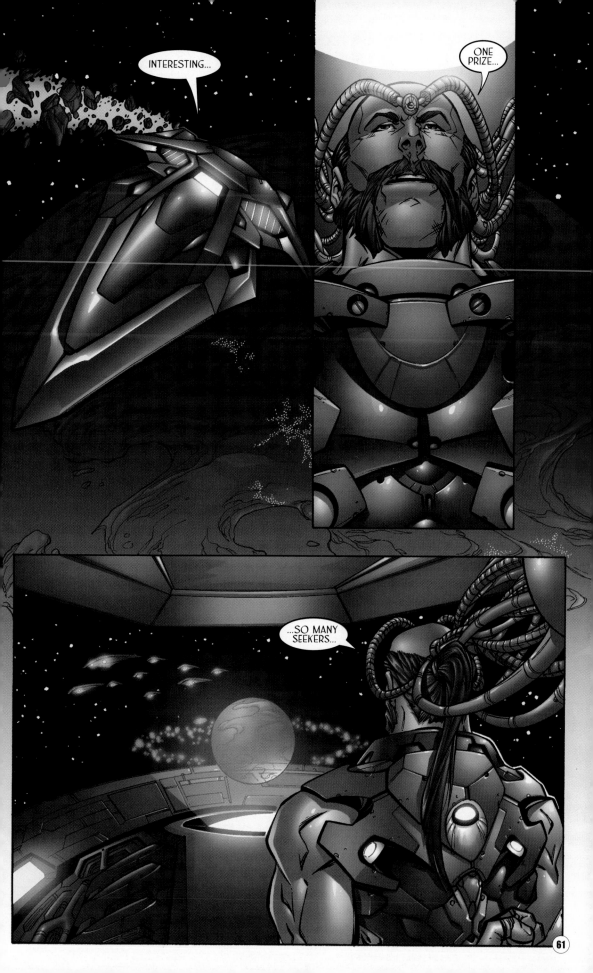

AW, ROI...

WE'VE BOTH SEEN DEATH A HUNDRED TIMES OVER, SO WHY'S THIS ONE SEEM SO... WRONG?

I GUESS I NEVER REALIZED HOW MUCH YOU MEANT TO ME UNTIL...

SAM, WE'RE OUT OF THE KEYHOLE.

SAM...?

SAM...

I'D BE LYING IF I DIDN'T SAY I'D RATHER STILL BE IN MY BODY THAN... HERE...

...BUT I'M HAPPY TO STILL BE AROUND.

MAYBE...

NO MAYBE ABOUT IT, ROI--

THE SAURS WILL PAY FOR THIS, DON'T YOU WORRY!

I MEANT MAYBE THERE'S A WAY TO PUT ME BACK TOGETHER.

SOMEHOW, THERE'S GOT TO BE AN *ACCOUNTING...*

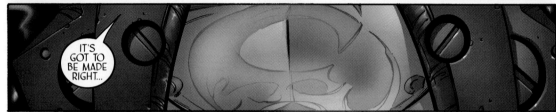

IT'S GOT TO BE MADE *RIGHT...*

YOU'VE GOT TO BE *AVENGED!*

VREEPVREEP

VREEPVREEP

WHA--?

THE DOORS WON'T CLOSE...? DID *I* DO THAT?

STAY PUT! I'M NOT GONNA HURT YOU!

GRAWWWR

AS LONG AS YOU RETURN THE COURTESY -- HEY, NOW!

GRAWWWWWRP

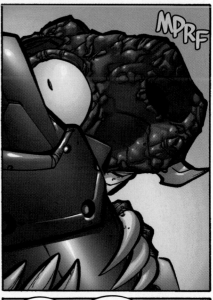

MPRF

AW, LOOKIT YOU...YOU'RE NO THREAT, ARE YA?

BESIDES, ROIYA LIKES YOU AND SHE'S HAD A TOUGH ENOUGH DAY.

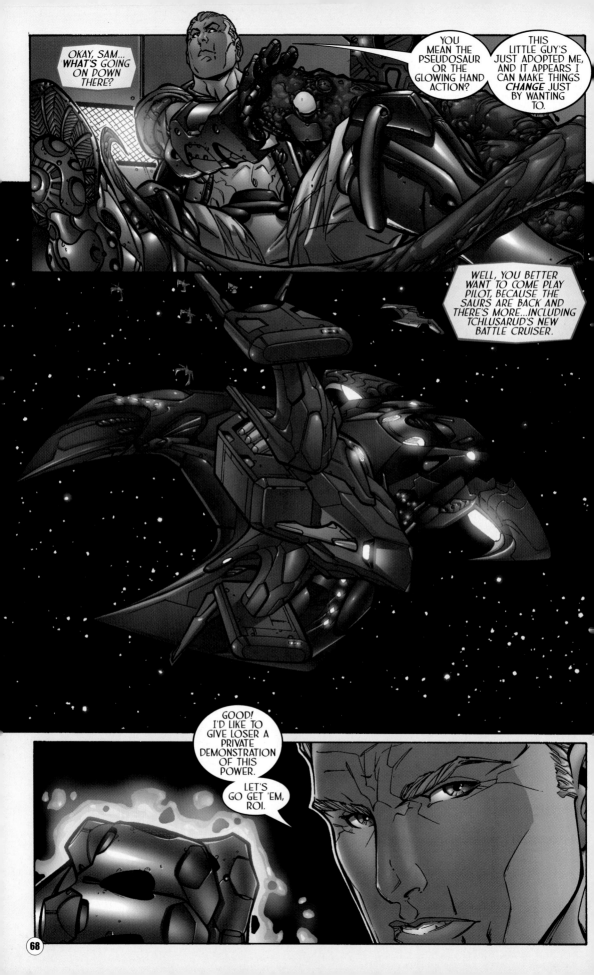

Chapter 3

"It reinforced the fact that in today's comic books, you can't rely on just the penciler to do great dynamic stuff to grab and hold on to a reader's attention — it's equal shares with the inker and the colorist."

– Wil Quintana

The United Colors of Comics

Sigil penciler Ben Lai and *Sigil* inker, brother Ray Lai, weren't quite sure what they were looking at.

Sigil writer Barbara Kesel brought to the office an old comic book from the 1970s to demonstrate some of the storytelling techniques of comics' "Silver Age" artists. But to the Lais, something didn't look right.

"It was the color," Barbara recalled. "Until that point, they had never seen a flat-colored comic before."

For the uninitiated, flat-color refers to a process by which basic colors, through the standard four-color process, were applied to comic books back in the early days. Before the advent of computers, comic books would be sent to the printing plant in black-and-white format along with a color guide to show the printer what was supposed to be blue, what was supposed to be red, and so forth. Most of the time, minimum-wage printing-plant pre-press artists would literally paint red glop onto plastic sheets which were then photographed through filters to generate the various "dot" levels for the four colors (YRBK, or yellow, red, blue, and black) in order to make Superman's shirt blue (B, or 100% blue) and his "S" shield red (YR, or 100% magenta and 100% yellow).

Today, with the advent of computers, it's possible for colorists to achieve a near-painted quality to their work

The Lai Brothers, having been fans primarily of Japanese *manga* (comic books) and comic books published by companies like Image, had never seen a standard four-color comic book in their lives.

"Ben and Ray were part of the first generation affected by the paradigm shift still taking place in comics today," proclaims Barbara. "It used

> **"It used to be that comic book art was considered *finished* after it was penciled and inked, and then it was sent out to be colored, as if the coloring wasn't really part of the art, just a final process. Ben and Ray represent a new generation that believes the art is not finished *until* it is colored."**

to be that comic book art was considered *finished* after it was penciled and inked, and then it was sent out to be colored, as if the coloring wasn't really part of the art, just a final process. Ben and Ray represent a new generation that believes the art is not finished *until* it is colored."

In a vacuum, that attitude alone would seem to pave the way for better comics. But it was the studio system CrossGen employs that added human interaction to the dazzling computer effects available to create the most synergistic situation possible.

"With the computer capabilities we have now, much of what appears on the final page goes beyond what was on the already terrific penciled and inked art," Barbara said. "Once again, having everybody in-house means that the three artists on each page can contribute fully to the communal process of creating that page. The penciler can set up an effect knowing what tools the colorist has to bring it to life, or even create additional levels to the page that exist as special effects to be imported by the colorist. The art on the page is no longer 'all there' before the coloring effects are completed."

Of course, that was an important point for *Sigil* colorist Wil Quintana. While he was already immersed in the process of computer coloring, Ben and Ray's attitude about colors affected Wil greatly because many of their pages left a great deal of room for a colorist's contributions. They counted on Wil to contribute to the look, mood, and feel of every page.

"They certainly made me feel like a more active participant in the whole creative process of the book," Wil said. "It reinforced the fact that in today's comic books, you can't rely on just the penciler to do great dynamic stuff to grab and hold on to a reader's attention – it's equal shares with the inker and the colorist."

"...I KNOW EXACTLY WHAT I'M DOIN'."

SAURIAN CUTWING FIGHTERS

SAURIAN BATTLE CRUISER
JAHKEMRAH

30 YEARS IN SERVICE
ARC DRIVE RETROFITTED
CREW: 2,100
SPACECRAFT:
 5-20 CUTWING FIGHTERS
 10 SHUTTLECRAFT
 2 HEAVY LANDERS

ROYAL SAURIAN
BATTLE CRUISER
MAKRUTHTE

2 YEARS IN SERVICE
ARC DRIVE EQUIPPED
CREW: 1,600
SPACECRAFT:
 10-50 CUTWING FIGHTERS
 10 SHUTTLECRAFT
 2 HEAVY LANDERS

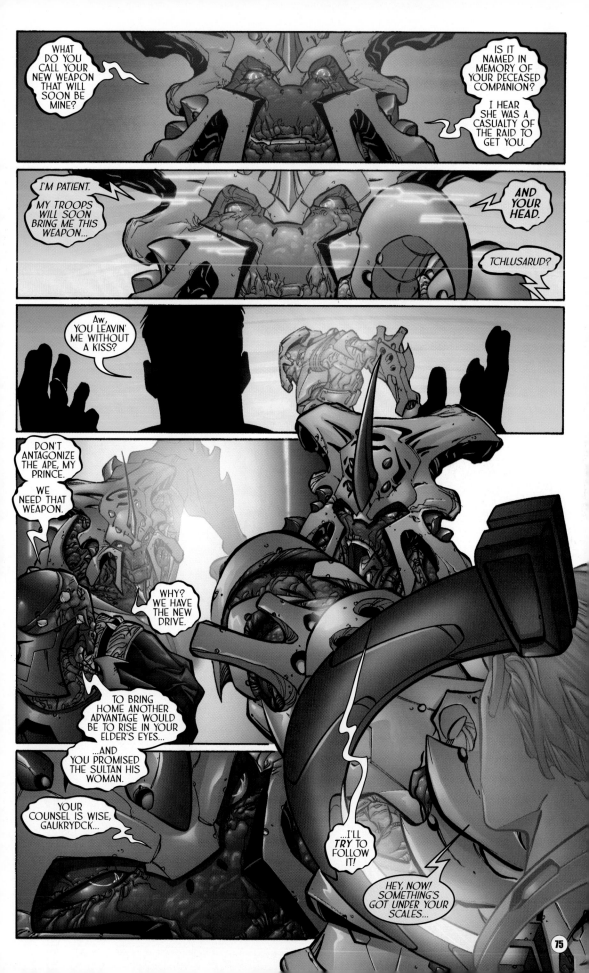

...TOO BAD I'M JUST A HOLO ON YOUR END.

THIS IS PRICELESS. LOSER'S IN A LATHER.

HE WANTS THAT BOMB AND HE'LL SEE TO KEEPING US SAFE UNTIL HE CAN GET HIS CLAWS ON IT...

...A WEAPON WE DON'T AND NEVER HAD.

Uh, SAM... YOU MAY BE A LITTLE WRONG ABOUT THAT.

I'VE BEEN RUNNING AN ANALYSIS OF THE ENERGY PATTERN OF THAT LITTLE TRICK YOU PULLED ON THE DOORS AGAINST THE DATA FROM THE BLAST ON TANIPAL.

IT'S A DEAD MATCH, SAM.

WE DO HAVE THE WEAPON...

IT'S YOU.

THE *BITTERLUCK* IS LICENSED TO SAMANDAHL REY WITH SURVIVOR'S RIGHTS LISTED TO ROIYA SINTOR...

...THE WOMAN WE'VE IDENTIFIED AS A CASUALTY OF THE SAURIAN ACTION YESTERDAY.

WITNESSES HAVE ALSO PLACED THE KIDNAPPED ZANNIATI ON THE *BITTERLUCK*...

...THE SHIP THAT LEFT TANIPAL AT THE HEART OF THE EXPLOSION.

WITHOUT SUSTAINING ANY DAMAGE FROM THE BLAST!

WE ASSUME THERE'S A CONNECTION, SULTAN RONOLO.

YOU CAN TELL YOUR MASTERS I DON'T HOLD THE PLANETARY UNION RESPONSIBLE, BUT I *DO* EXPECT YOUR ASSISTANCE APPREHENDING REY.

ALSO, MY GUARDS OBSERVED A SECOND MALE...

WHO WAS IDENTIFIED AS ONE OF YOUR OWN GUARDS...

"CORRECT. HE WAS OBSERVED TOUCHING MY WIFE..."

77

"AND WE BAIL WHILE THEY HIT THE KEYHOLE...

"...WHOSE COURSE IS SET TO BOOMERANG."

WATCH THAT SAURIAN BATTLER, NOW...

TRANSIT POINT OPENING! *CALL ALERT!* SHIELDS UP!

"...'CAUSE THOSE SAURS ARE ABOUT TO RECEIVE SOME FRIENDLY FIRE!"

MY PRINCE! OUR SENSORS SHOW NO SIGN OF DAMAGE... ...BUT WE HAVE DECOMPRESSION ON THE MAIN LEVEL! SHOULD I ORDER THE FIGHTERS TO RETURN?

NO. I WANT TO END THIS SITUATION MYSELF.

TEN YEARS' PAY TO THE ONE WHO DELIVERS THE HUMAN TO ME!

HREEEEN

GREENK

HRMMMMMMMMMM

HEY THERE, LOSER.

Chapter 4

"Sam's the first hero to come along in his universe in a while. There's a war that's been going on for so long, and the humans there are so beaten down, that they can barely bring the idea of a hero to mind."

— *Barbara Kesel*

Triad of Intrigue

While many comic books tend to use other comic books as reference points and inspiration, CrossGen's approach was different. While our direction owes a lot to comic books from the past, it also owes a lot to more broad-ranging cultural and classical influences.

For *Sigil* writer Barbara Kesel, mythology and classic heroic literature serve as her muses.

"Classic structure seems to create a triangle of three: hero, warrior, and jester," explained Barbara. "We used this structure in *Sigil*, setting up the triangle of Roiya, Sam, and JeMerik, but not in the roles you might initially expect. *Roiya* was set up as the hero, not Sam. That's a classic fallacy with stories in this genre. People think that the lead character is automatically the hero when, in fact, other characters may possess more inherently heroic characteristics. Now, the hero – Roiya – gets killed in chapter one, so the guy who is used to being the back-up, the fighter who just kicks butt when he's told to kick butt, must suddenly take on the role of hero. This doesn't mean he's suited to it – he's just placed in it, with the other two (one, granted, in 'spirit' form) to guide him along."

The wild card here is JeMerik Meer, who in this triad takes the role of jester. Below is the actual character description written by Barbara way back in 1999, many months before issue #1 of *Sigil* hit the stands.

"JEMERIK MEER: A tall, stylish fashion plate with short gold-white curls

---

"JeMerik is just the kind of guy who would make Sam crazy. He's young, good-looking, he has the easy job, and things always seem to fall into place for him. He is everything that Sam might really have wanted to be but never had the chance."

---

and a glowing smile hiding his scheming mind, JeMerik is clearly the most good-looking man of the bunch. He loves to flirt, to charm, to laugh, to enjoy life. He is both enjoyable and a nuisance. Since his main form of supporting himself is to sponge off others, he travels very light. He carries a small shoulder pack with his vital belongings; a bag that always seems to have just what he needs to salvage any situation. His strange

orange eyes mark him as unusual."

Barbara liked JeMerik because he became a classic foil for Sam's tough-guy persona.

"JeMerik is just the kind of guy who would make Sam crazy," Barbara said. "He's young, good-looking, he has the easy job, and things always seem to fall into place for him. He is everything that Sam might really have wanted to be but never had the chance."

So with the role switcheroo, Sam finds himself with the power to perhaps tap the hidden potential within himself – if he can only overcome all the cynicism and bitterness that having a guy like JeMerik around brings out in him.

"Sam's the first hero to come along in his universe in a while," Barbara said. "There's a war that's been going on for so long, and the humans there are so beaten down, that they can barely bring the idea of a hero to mind. In one sense JeMerik seems to be goading Sam, but in the long run, it's just the thing that Sam needs to realize that it takes more than strength and power to be a hero; it takes strength of one's convictions and an enormous amount of will-

ZANNI, *BREATHE.*

EVEN IF YOU DO MAKE OPEN SPACE...

...WE'RE IN THE LEFT END OF NOWHERE.

YOU'D NEVER BE FOUND.

IT'S A BETTER CHANCE THAN I HAVE NOW. PLEASE LET ME IN.

NO, ZANNI. YOU'D JUST BE THROWING YOUR LIFE AWAY...

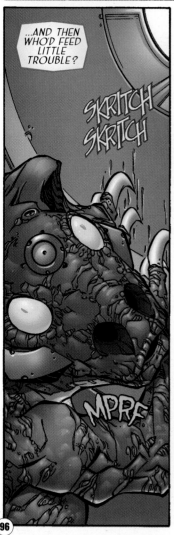

...AND THEN WHO'D FEED LITTLE *TROUBLE?*

SKRITCH SKRITCH

MPRF

YOU'RE... *RIGHT.*

THERE MUST BE ANOTHER WAY...

...I COULD...

USE THAT GUN ON THE *SAURIANS?*

...YES.

YES.

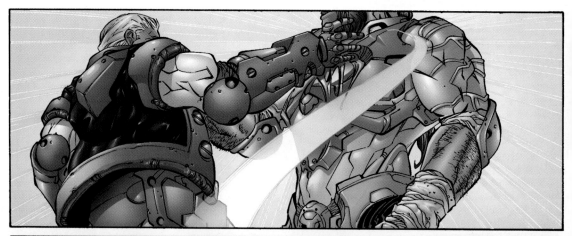

INTERESTING... TRANSMUTATION OF NON-BIOLOGIC MATERIAL...

...SIMILAR TO BRAAG'S ABILITY.

YOU CAN SAVE YOUR ENERGY, HUMAN --

-- YOUR POWER DOESN'T MEAN A THING TO ME.

SKREEE

JeMERIK, I THOUGHT YOU SAID YOU'D LEAD THEM AWAY FROM ME!

I THOUGHT I COULD...

YOU TWO MIGHT WANT TO MOVE...

JUST LIKE A LIZARD -- CUT A HOLE THROUGH MY SIDE WHEN THE DOOR'S NOT LOCKED...

PFSSSHT

LOOK OUT!

PARDON ME!

FWOOSH

I ALSO THOUGHT THEY'D USE THE AIRLOCK.

IT'S NOT AS BAD AS IT LOOKS, ZANNI.

YOU'LL BE SAFE... ...I KEPT YOU ALIVE FOR A REASON!

NO, THAT'S NOT--

NO.

THAT'S *NOT*.

I *WILL* NOT LET THAT HAPPEN.

PaCHOOM PaCHOOM

VIOLET OCULAR DISPLAY!

DON'T FIRE! THAT ONE'S A NO-KILL!

PaCHOOM

PaCHOOM PaCHOOM

PaCHOOM

KLAK KLAK

YOU WON'T GO BACK TO THE SULTAN, ZANNI. *TRUST* ME.

JeMERIK, I'M ALL OUT OF TRUST.

I WAS BEGINNING TO THINK I COULD TRUST SAM, AND WHERE IS HE NOW?

IN TROUBLE AGAIN, OF COURSE, BUT SAM SEEMS TO BE AS GOOD AT GETTING HIMSELF *OUT* OF TROUBLE AS IN...

GRAWWWWWRRR

PSEUDOSAUR!

IT'S *CRAZED!* I'LL ELIMINATE IT.

IT'S ONLY A PET! SAVE YOUR AMMO FOR THE *APES...*

"...OR *US* -- ONCE WE FACE THE PRINCE AND TELL HIM WE'VE FOUND *NOTHING* ABOARD."

THE ONLY LIVING BEINGS ON THIS SHIP ARE HERE IN THIS CHAMBER.

DISTURBING.

AT LEAST THE SULTAN RONOLO WILL BE PLEASED BY THE RETURN OF THE WIFE WHO BROKE CONTRACT AND FLED.

I HAVE THE *RIGHT* TO PROTECT MY OWN LIFE.

HUMAN, *YOU* ARE ANNOYING BUT NECESSARY.

THE OTHER IS NOT.

THE SULTAN WISHES HIM ELIMINATED.

THROW HIM FROM THE SHIP.

WHAT?!

BEGGING YOUR INDULGENCE, YOUR HIGHNESS, BUT YOU'RE MAKING A TERRIBLE MISTAKE.

YOU SAY THE SULTAN WANTS HIM DEAD...

...BUT JEMERIK MEER IS MORE THAN HE APPEARS TO BE...

...YOU MIGHT BE SACRIFICING A VALUABLE RESOURCE, LEVERAGE TO USE AGAINST RONOLO...

...DON'T YOU WANT TO TAKE A MOMENT TO THINK IT OVER...

...BEFORE I RIP OPEN YOUR GILL SACS?

OR ARE YOU IMMUNE TO YOUR OWN POISONS?

WE LOST *HOW* MANY SHIPS?

OKAY, *WHO* WANTS TO SUMMARIZE FOR MAIN BASE? CROSS?

Oh, ALL RIGHT.

FOR THE RECORD. RECORDING *ON*.

BEGIN REPORT, MISTER CROSS.

HONNA INCIDENT, *FACTS*:

THE EXPLOSION LEFT NO HEAT, NO RADIATION, NO EVIDENCE EXCEPT FOR ITS SPHERE OF DESTRUCTION.

THIS UNIDENTIFIED WEAPON IS SOMEHOW LINKED TO SAMANDAHL REY, OWNER OF THE *BITTERLUCK*, WHICH LEFT TANIPAL WITH AT LEAST TWO HUMAN PASSENGERS.

REY'S SHIP IS NOW IN THE POSSESSION OF TCHLUSARUD, SO WE CAN ASSUME THAT THE SAURIANS HAVE THE WEAPON...

...ABOUT WHICH WE STILL HAVE NO USEFUL DATA.

RECORDING *OFF*.

WE CAN'T LOSE THAT WEAPON TO THE SAURS.

VINZER, DO YOU STILL HAVE SOMEONE ON TCHARUN?

THAT I DO.

I'LL SEE WHAT HE CAN FIND OUT.

114

Chapter 5

"When the costumes were initially being designed, the Lai brothers brought in a heavy *manga* influence, as this is what they were familiar with. *Manga*-style science fiction is very popular in Japan, and it's distinguished by a certain ruggedness, a sense of bulk and equipment. I think Sam's costume reflects those sensibilities."

– *Brandon Peterson*

And on the seventh day...

According to the book of Genesis, it took God seven days to create the universe.

For the CrossGen Brain Trust of Mark Alessi, Gina Villa, Barbara Kesel, Ron Marz, and Brandon Peterson, it took the better part of two days to create the worlds of *Sigil*. Maybe it was the whole "multiple planet" thing that cost them the extra time.

"Well, I started thinking about things in the car when I was driving cross-country to move to Florida," Barbara said. "Then there were five days of conferences in-house, where the gist of every book got created, and then I would write up specific character, world, and setting descriptions and give them to the artists. During that process on *Sigil*, the Lai brothers sometimes discovered something new that they liked and threw it back my way until the Powers That Be were satisfied with the Lais' design work. Seven days to create a universe? Creating the specific worlds and locales for *CrossGenesis*, our first preview comic, took a couple of weeks. So, creating the whole universe took about two months."

One of the more collaborative efforts was the design of the costumes for the main characters. CrossGen art director Brandon Peterson supervised the Lai brothers as they worked on the look and feel of *Sigil*'s cast of characters.

"When the costumes were initially being designed, the Lai brothers brought in a heavy *manga* influence, as this is what they were familiar with," Brandon said. "*Manga*-style science fiction is very

---

"Now, unlike standard superhero books, these characters' clothing was functional, and so defining a look for them that could be consistent through clothing changes and several different settings through the first story arc was difficult, especially when the incidental characters were dressed in similar fashions."

---

popular in Japan, and it's distinguished by a certain ruggedness, a sense of bulk and equipment. I think Sam's costume reflects those sensibilities. Sam almost looks military with his Spartan lack of decoration, but his initial costume also has elements of a very futuristic armor."

One of the pillars of the CrossGen Universe is that our characters will not be as tied to "costumes" in the classic sense of super-hero comic book characters. CrossGen's characters change their clothes just like normal people, and it was more important initially for the art teams to develop a style and a look than it was a specific costume for a specific character.

"Roiya's initial costume matched a lot of Sam's lines in design," Brandon explained. "She was in the same type of work as a soldier-of-fortune, so that made sense. Later, that changed somewhat. JeMerik's look was radically different from theirs in its use of cloth instead of metal. Zanni, on the other hand, initially wore a costume that suited her appearance but not necessarily her character. Zanni was created as an exotic beauty, and she had to wear this harem outfit because she was one of the Sultan's wives. However, it won't be her style as the story progresses. Now, unlike standard super-hero books, these characters' clothing was functional, and so defining a look for them that could be consistent through clothing changes and several different settings through the first story arc was difficult, especially when the incidental characters were dressed in similar fashions. In reading through the book, I think we were successful in that the characters remained easily identifiable."

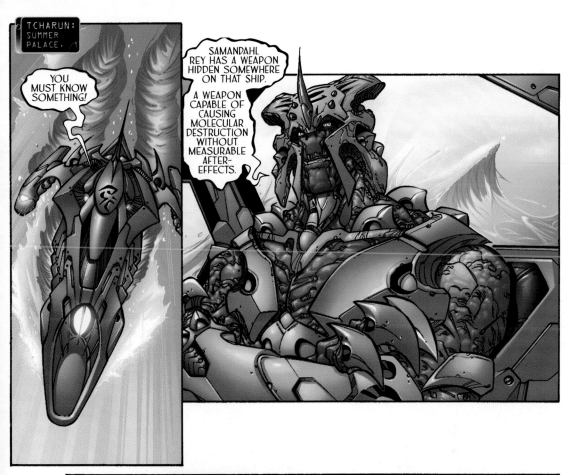

YOU MUST KNOW SOMETHING!

SAMANDAHL REY HAS A WEAPON HIDDEN SOMEWHERE ON THAT SHIP.

A WEAPON CAPABLE OF CAUSING MOLECULAR DESTRUCTION WITHOUT MEASURABLE AFTER-EFFECTS.

AND YET YOU KNOW *NOTHING* OF HIS LOCATION, OR *WHAT* OR *WHERE* THAT *WEAPON* MIGHT BE!

MY TECHNICIANS ARE ALREADY SCRUTINIZING REY'S SHIP FOR ANSWERS.

UNFORTUNATELY, I CANNOT LET THEM DO THE SAME TO *YOU.*

SO YOU WILL REMAIN IN MY... GUEST QUARTERS UNTIL I CAN ARRANGE FOR YOUR RETURN TO YOUR LOVING HUSBAND.

PERHAPS YOU WILL REFLECT ON YOUR HUSBAND'S REACTION TO YOUR...

...ADVENTURE...

...WITH SAMANDAHL REY.

I'M SURE HE CANNOT WAIT TO SHOW YOU JUST HOW PLEASED HE IS WITH YOUR...

...INITIATIVE.

WHAT A CLUMSY ATTEMPT AT AN OBLIQUE HINT.

IT WAS A SAD DAY WHEN YOU LIZARDS STOPPED GRUNTING AND BEGAN SPEAKING OUR LANGUAGE.

YOU KNOW RONOLO LIKES TO INFLICT PAIN, TCHLUSARUD.

HE SIMPLY DOES IT WITH BLOWS, NOT INNUENDO.

RRRRAGAIN, YOUR STATUS SAVES YOU FROM YOURSELF.

FOR YOUR SAFETY, ALSO, A SMALL DEMONSTRATION OF OUR SECURITY SYSTEM...

...GUARD?...

...USING A SMALL MAMMAL LIKE YOURSELF.

CLNNNK

CHEE!

CHEE! CHEE!

A GOOD HOST MAKES HIS GUEST AWARE OF ALL POTENTIAL DANGERS.

IN CASE YOU WERE ENTERTAINING THOUGHTS OF... WANDERING...

CHEE! CHEE!

"...KNOW THAT IT WILL COME WITH A PRICE.

SPLOOSH

"THAT PRICE IS PAIN AND PROBABLE DEATH."

SHOULD YOU NEED ANYTHING TO MAKE YOUR WAIT HERE MORE COMFORTABLE, *HONORED* ZANNIATI, MY GUARDS WILL PROVIDE.

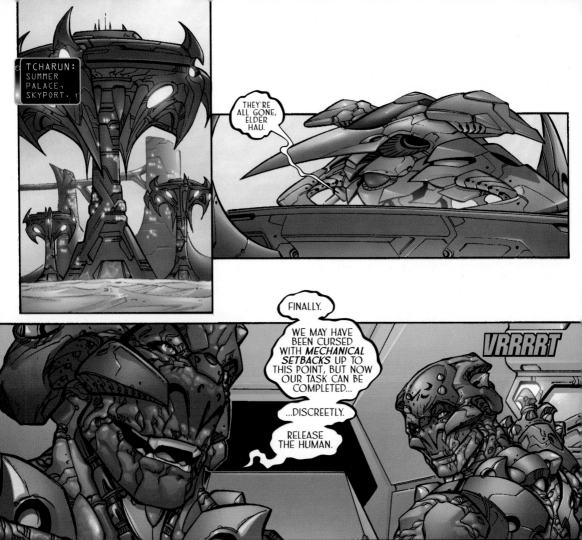

TCHARUN: SUMMER PALACE, SKYPORT.

THEY'RE ALL GONE, ELDER HAU.

FINALLY.

WE MAY HAVE BEEN CURSED WITH *MECHANICAL SETBACKS* UP TO THIS POINT, BUT NOW OUR TASK CAN BE COMPLETED...

...DISCREETLY.

RELEASE THE HUMAN.

VRRRRT

PERHAPS WE CAN ACTUALLY KILL IT THIS TIME.

ELDER HAU--

WHERE IS IT?

LOOKING FOR *ME?*

IT'S AMAZING HOW THINGS GO WRONG FOR YOU TWO.

AIRLOCKS THAT WON'T OPEN, WEAPONS THAT HOLD NO CHARGE...

KRANGK

KRAK

IT'S ALMOST AS IF YOU WEREN'T MEANT TO KILL ME...

...ALTHOUGH I DON'T THINK TCHLUSARUD WOULD WELCOME THAT EXPLANATION.

SORRY I CAN'T OFFER YOU...

...A BETTER ONE!

NO, BAJOUNTE-KA!

DON'T BOTHER WITH THE APE...

"...THOSE ARE DANGEROUS WATERS..."

SPLOOSH

125

"...HE'S DONE FOR."

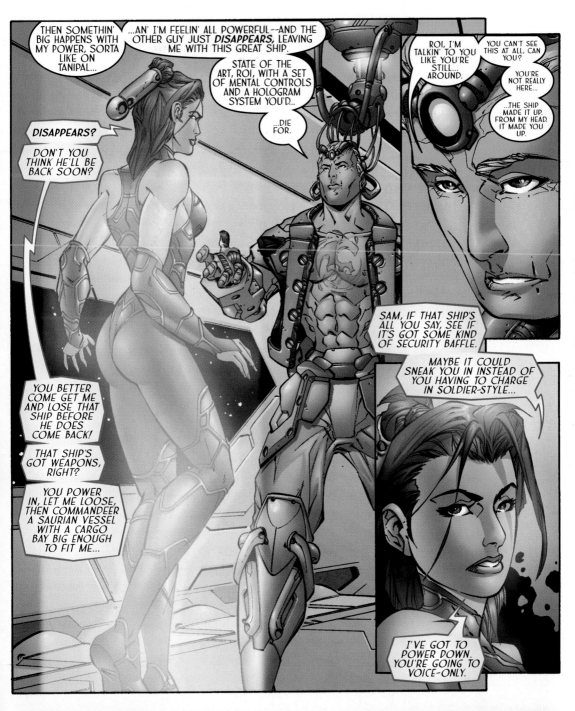

THEN SOMETHIN' BIG HAPPENS WITH MY POWER, SORTA LIKE ON TANIPAL...

...AN' I'M FEELIN' ALL POWERFUL--AND THE OTHER GUY JUST *DISAPPEARS,* LEAVING ME WITH THIS GREAT SHIP.

STATE OF THE ART, ROI, WITH A SET OF MENTAL CONTROLS AND A HOLOGRAM SYSTEM YOU'D...

...DIE FOR.

ROI, I'M TALKIN' TO YOU LIKE YOU'RE STILL... AROUND.

YOU CAN'T SEE THIS AT ALL, CAN YOU?

YOU'RE NOT REALLY HERE...

...THE SHIP MADE IT UP. FROM MY HEAD. IT MADE YOU UP.

DISAPPEARS?

DON'T YOU THINK HE'LL BE BACK SOON?

SAM, IF THAT SHIP'S ALL YOU SAY, SEE IF IT'S GOT SOME KIND OF SECURITY BAFFLE.

MAYBE IT COULD SNEAK YOU IN INSTEAD OF YOU HAVING TO CHARGE IN SOLDIER-STYLE...

YOU BETTER COME GET ME AND LOSE THAT SHIP BEFORE HE DOES COME BACK!

THAT SHIP'S GOT WEAPONS, RIGHT?

YOU POWER IN, LET ME LOOSE, THEN COMMANDEER A SAURIAN VESSEL WITH A CARGO BAY BIG ENOUGH TO FIT ME...

I'VE GOT TO POWER DOWN. YOU'RE GOING TO VOICE-ONLY.

HOW'S OUR OTHER NEW CREW? I DON'T SEE THEM...

LOSER'S GOT ZANNIATI, SAM...

...AND I'M NOT SURE IF JEMERIK'S STILL ALIVE.

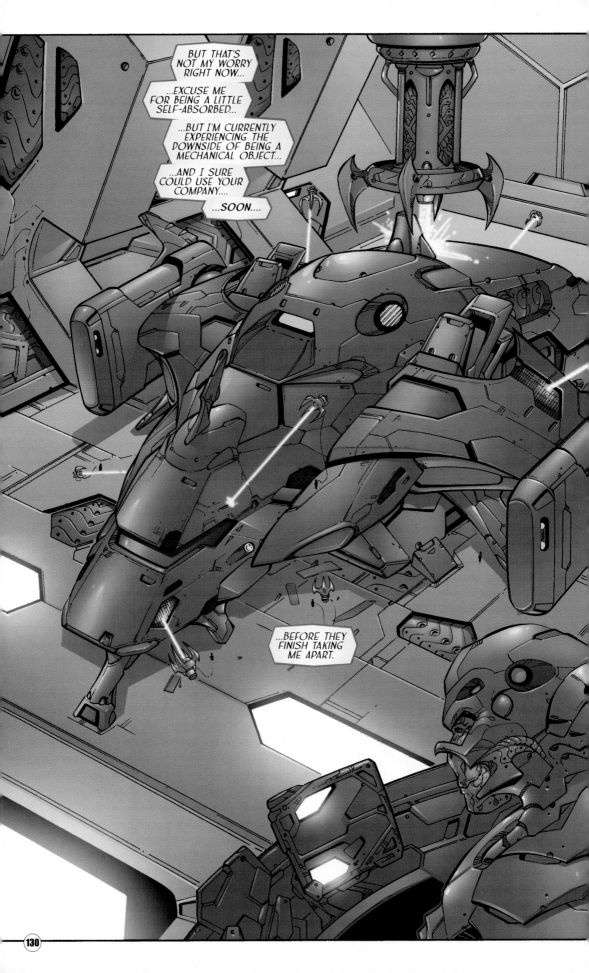

TCHARUN: SHOPPING DISTRICT.

J.O. SEEHEY
PURVEYOR OF EXOTIC MEATS
Cuts for Festive Gatherings a Specialty

"THAT'S COST PER KILO...

...WE CAN ALSO PREPARE PACKAGES IN BULK, WITH AN APPROPRIATE DISCOUNT.

JAYO-SEEHEY-KA, THIS WAS JUST DELIVERED...

EXCUSE ME, PLEASE...

...THIS IS PRIVATE.

FAMILY MATTERS...

FAMILY OF *MAN.*

VRTT! JUST A HEADS UP, J.O. -- THE SULTAN'S MISSING WIFE IS ON HER WAY TO TCHARUN.

HOLO FILE ATTACHED.

THE RELATIONSHIP BETWEEN THE SAURIANS AND THE SULTAN WOULD BE *DAMAGED* IF ANYTHING *UNFORTUNATE* HAPPENED TO THE WOMAN...

...THOUGHT *YOU* SHOULD BE WARNED THAT RONOLO WOULD BLAME THE SAURIANS IF *TRAGEDY* STRUCK.

I GET THE MESSAGE.

HAS THE SULTAN BEEN INFORMED THAT WE HAVE HIS MISSING PROPERTY?

YES, SECOND INHERITOR. SULTAN RONOLO IS SENDING A SHIP TO RETRIEVE THE WOMAN.

NO, *I* WILL SPEAK. THE BLAME IS MINE.

HONORED TCHLUSARUD!

WE REGRET TO INFORM YOU THAT WE INITIALLY FAILED TO KILL THE HUMAN MALE.

THERE WERE EQUIPMENT MALFUNCTIONS... WE DID NOT WISH TO BURDEN YOU...

THE HUMAN IS VERY HARD TO KILL.

IT ESCAPED A SECOND TIME, BUT--

WHAT?!

YOU MISERABLE FAILURES LET IT ESCAPE ON TCHARUN?

JeMERIK'S ALIVE...

LET ME SHOW YOU HOW EASY IT IS TO **KILL!**

GYAA H

GYAGRGE

GLGL

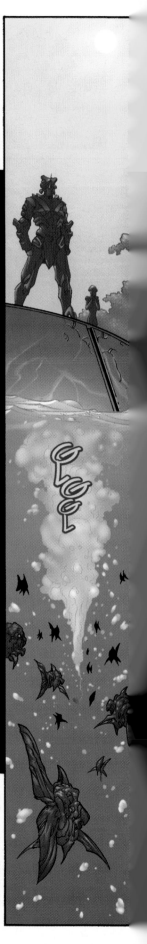

HONORED ELDER! THE HUMAN!

WE BELIEVE IT IS NOW DEAD, AS IT DOVE INTO THE WATERS WHERE THE *SENTINEL* DWELLS! THERE WAS *TURBULENCE...*

WE FAILED TO FOLLOW YOUR DIRECT ORDERS, HONORED TCHLUSARUD...

...BUT WE DID ACHIEVE THE OBJECTIVE! MY MOST HUMBLE APOLOGY FOR OUR UNACCEPTABLE BEHAVIOR!

TO WHICH MY IMPATIENT RESPONSE HAS NOW CAUSED A WASTE OF GOOD EXPERIENCE...

=SIGH= I MUST WORK MORE WITH THE WEAPONSMASTER.

THESE CONTINUING LOSSES OF CONTROL ARE... UNACCEPTABLE.

POOR JeMERIK, POOR ROIYA...

Oh, SAM...

...WHERE ARE YOU?

"...MOOT POINT IF I DON'T PASS THEIR SECURITY CHECK."

YOU ARE ENTERING ORBITOWER SECURED SPACE. STAND BY FOR CLEARANCE...

...SHUTTLE T-ZERO-THREE CLEARED FOR BERTH SEVEN-FOUR.

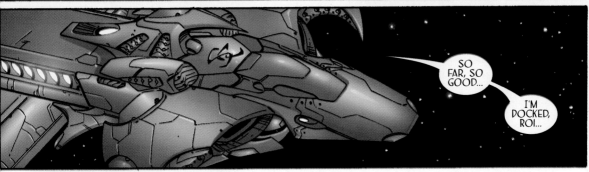

SO FAR, SO GOOD...

I'M DOCKED, ROI...

...SEE YOU SOON.

KFFFSSSHH

WHA--?

AN APE? HERE?

AFTER I BREAK THE GRAPPLE, YOU GET OUT OF HERE AND HIDE.

THE DARK MOON-- KEEP TO ITS FAR SIDE AND WE'LL RENDEZVOUS THERE ONCE I GRAB MY SHIP AND--

SAM?

WERE YOU PLANNING TO GO GET ZANNIATI?

AFTER I GET *YOU* FREE AND FULLY REPAIRED, THEN I'LL--

DO IT FIRST.

ZANNI HELPED US OUT AND NOW SHE'S IN TROUBLE. I CAN'T GET AROUND THAT.

YOU'VE GOT THAT HOT SHIP...

...I'LL WAIT.

NOW, ROI...

...YOU TRYIN' TO PLAY HERO ON ME?

WHO'S THE ONE WITH THE POWERS HERE? SEEMS TO ME HERO'S *YOUR* JOB.

SEE YA, SOLDIER.

BRACE FOR VACUUM...

Chapter 6

"That issue of *Sigil* was my first full comic book story... definitely a trial by fire."

– *Steve McNiven*

The Revenge of Steve

The award-winning author and playwright George Bernard Shaw once said, "He who can, does. He who cannot, teaches."

Well, Steve McNiven isn't that cynical. For Steve, a staff penciler at CrossGen and fill-in penciler for the chapter you've just read, it was quite the reverse from Shaw's rule. Steve was an art teacher who turned in his chalkboard for a drawing table at CrossGen and never looked back.

For Steve, it all started in July of 1999. He attended a comic book convention in San Diego and dropped off some samples at the CrossGen booth even though CrossGen hadn't begun publishing yet – it was the company's first appearance at Comic-Con International.

"I got a call from [CrossGen CEO] Mark Alessi just as school was starting, and we talked," Steve recalled. "He sent me down a test plot, which I turned around and sent back in mid-October 1999. Not long after that, I got the offer to be an associate penciler, which meant doing fill-in work and training to maybe someday take over the monthly penciling chores on a CrossGen comic book. By January of 2000, I'd moved my family from Canada to Tampa, Florida."

Now the full-time penciler on *Meridian*, another CrossGen Comics monthly title (available at all comic shops everywhere!), Steve took a major step in his new career with the previous chapter of this book.

"That issue of *Sigil* was my first full comic book story, complete with cover and all, so I was trying to iron things out, trying to perfect everything from storytelling to rendering –

> **"It was fun working with those characters. I loved the action and the energy in the book... in the end, I really think that we stayed true to the material and to the story."**

definitely a trial by fire," Steve said.

Still true to his teacher roots, Steve was also his own harshest critic.

"I think parts of it turned out well, but there is some stuff that makes me cringe a little," Steve chuckled. "Now, a lot of people say that's supposed to be good, looking back on something you've done and deciding it's not as good as you wanted. It means you're progressing, but man! It's still a bit painful!"

Still, Steve's cover to *Sigil* #6 (reproduced without logos on page 141 of this volume) has become one of the hallmark images of the first story arc. But interpreting Sam and his battle with the Saurians in the initial sequence of that issue, a scene Steve found particularly enjoyable, was a bit daunting.

"It was fun working with those characters," he said. "I loved the action and the energy in the book. One of the harder things to tackle, though, was the outfitting and weaponry of the characters. One of the strengths of Ben Lai, *Sigil*'s original penciler, was that he knew how to design 'tech-ware.' He simply had a knack for doing those sorts of things, and it was very hard to follow up on that. He had a way of making things work that was hard to duplicate, but in the end, I really think that we stayed true to the material and to the story."

Sigil writer Barbara Kesel, a former editor at publishers DC and Dark Horse, also took some pride in Steve's initial work because it afforded her the opportunity to predict where Steve's talents would be best utilized.

"This issue was his first full story, and through all the science fiction trappings, equipment and techno-stuff, I saw little nuances in Steve's style that made me think he would be a perfect fit for *Meridian*," Barbara said. "Time – and the fans – have proven me right on this one." ↻

145

BROKE YOUR--? YOU'RE TELLING ME YOU'RE STANDING IN VACUUM WITH NO HEADGEAR?

THAT, OR I'M DEAD AN' DREAMIN'.

BUT THIS DREAM'S GOT SAUR GUARDS INSTEADA YOU IN IT...

...SO I SUSPECT I'M AWAKE.

NOT GOOD.

BACK-UPS?

NOPE, BIGGER PROBLEM...

...SAURIAN SECURITY SHIP.

TWO-PHASE PLASMA CANNONS... GET THE HELL OUT OF THERE, SAM. THEY'LL FRY THEIR OWN TO GET YOU.

THAT THOUGHT HAD CROSSED MY MIND.

Oh, YEAH-- IT'S ALWAYS YOUR IDEA.

F'COURSE!

WHAT A SORRY BUNCHA TUMBLEDOWN TROOPERS!

BUT WHEN THEY REPORT THIS TO THEIR BOSS, THEY BETTER MAKE ME LOOK GOOD...

BUT I TELL YA, ROI -- MAKIN' THINGS MOVE, NOT NEEDIN' AIR TO BREATHE -- IT'S ALL SOMETHING THAT NEEDS THINKING ABOUT.

MEANING?

I JUST KEEP THINKIN' THAT WHOEVER PLANTED THIS THING ON ME'S GONNA SHOW UP AND TAKE IT BACK.

AFTER ALL, WHO'D GIVE A TIRED-OUT SOLDIER A WEAPON LIKE THIS ON PURPOSE?

SOMEBODY WITH A GOOD EYE FOR POTENTIAL.

OR TWO BLIND ONES.

GO AHEAD AND LAUGH, ROI -- I'LL FIND A WAY TO GET YOU BACK BREATHIN' SOMEDAY...

...JUST SO'S I CAN KICK YOUR BUTT.

WHY?

WHY'S IT ALL SO?

WHY ME?

I AM CERTAIN YOU WILL BE COMFORTABLE UNTIL MY RETURN, HONORED ZANNIATI.

I REGRET THAT YOU HAD TO WITNESS MY UNFORTUNATE DISPLAY OF PUNISHMENT.

BUT I TRUST THAT YOU FULLY UNDERSTAND WHAT MIGHT BEFALL YOU SHOULD YOU TRY TO LEAVE THIS ESTATE.

YOU TWO! YOU WILL ACCOMPANY ME TO THE WEAPONSMASTER.

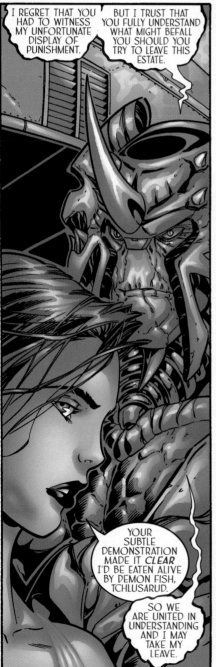

YOUR SUBTLE DEMONSTRATION MADE IT *CLEAR* I'D BE EATEN ALIVE BY DEMON FISH, TCHLUSARUD.

SO WE ARE UNITED IN UNDERSTANDING AND I MAY TAKE MY LEAVE.

WE'RE UNITED IN MORE THAN YOU KNOW, *LOSER*...

...WE *BOTH* KNOW YOUR SECRETS.

WHREEEEEEEEEN

I'M MAKING YOU TWO NERVOUS, AREN'T I?

WHREEEEN

YOU THINK YOU'RE GOING TO HAVE TO FOLLOW ME INTO THESE WATERS.

YOU CAN RELAX.

I WOULDN'T WANT TO SPOIL THE SULTAN'S REVENGE ON ME THAT WAY.

SPLOOOOOSH

I'LL FIND SOME OTHER WAY TO ESCAPE.

EH?

WHAT WAS *THAT!*

WAAHOOO!

CARE FOR A RIDE?

NOT YOU LIZARDS -- JUST THE GIRL.

JeMERIK?

DIVE IN! THIS SWEETHEART'S SCARED THE CARNIVORES AWAY!

C'MON -- IT'S SAFE!

I KNOW, I KNOW -- TRUST YOU.

NO! I HATE THIS JOB.

SPLOOSH

SO, JUST WHERE IS THIS WILD RIDE GOING?

SAURIAN SPACEPORT. WE'LL STEAL THE SHIP WE FLEW IN ON.

BUT YOU WEREN'T WITH ME...

GOTCHA, PRETTY LADY!

YES, I WAS. I RODE INSIDE THE BAGGAGE COMPARTMENT.

I WANT A WINDOW SEAT THIS TRIP.

NOW THERE'S SOMETHING YOU DON'T SEE.

I KINDA LIKE YOU TWO.

TOO BAD YOU'RE NOTHING BUT FRESH MEAT FOR THE BUTCHER SHOP.

TCHARUN: SUMMER PALACE, SKYPORT.

THEY DIDN'T.

I'VE BEEN EAVESDROPPING ON THE SULTAN'S COMM CHANNELS.

PRETTY EASY CODE TO BREAK.

ROI, YOU SAY THIS PLACE IS IT?

WHY WOULD THEY BE WILLING T'TELL YOU WHERE ZANNI WAS EXACTLY?

TOO LATE.

I STILL SAY THE ELEVATOR WOULD HAVE BEEN FASTER AND EASIER.

THIS IS SAFER.

ELECTRONICS HAVE A WAY OF BETRAYING YOUR POSITION.

CODE-BREAKIN' NOW?

WATCH YOURSELF, ROI.

I'VE GOT PRIVATE FILES STASHED IN THAT SHIP.

YOU STAY OUTTA 'EM.

NICE SAVE.

DOES THIS MEAN YOU'RE HERE TO REUNITE US WITH THE LOVELY ROIYA?

IN A SHORT WHILE. I'VE GOT ME SOME UNFINISHED BUSINESS WITH A CERTAIN SAURIAN PRINCE.

YOU TWO HOP INTO MY SHUTTLE HERE --

-- NEVER MIND ITS SHAPE --

-- AND I'LL BE BACK WITH YOU IN A HEARTBEAT.

SAM, IS THIS JUST FOR REVENGE? WHAT GOOD WILL IT DO... ROIYA IF YOU...?

I'LL BE BACK, ZANNI. THAT'S A PROMISE.

JUST GIVE ME AN HOUR TO FIND LOSER, WILLYA?

I... KNOW WHERE YOU SHOULD LOOK.

I HEARD HIM SAY HE WAS GOING TO SEE THE WEAPONSMASTER.

DOES THAT HELP?

THAT TELLS ME *EXACTLY* WHERE TO FIND HIM.

THE BLADE ARENA.

THIS WON'T TAKE LONG AT ALL.

YOU KNOW, *I* DOVE IN AMONG FLESH-EATING CREATURES TO SAVE YOU AND I DIDN'T GET A LOOK LIKE THAT.

THE FORMS ARE NOT YOUR BETRAYER, TCHLUSARUD.

IT IS YOUR ANIMAL SELF THAT MUST BE CONTROLLED.

REVIEW THE FORMS.

BEGIN WITH *FOCUS.*

BREATHE...

...RELAX YOUR STANCE...

...SHIFT YOUR WEIGHT FROM THE TALONS ONTO THE FOOTMASS...

PATIENCE.

CLOSE YOUR EYES...

...ENVISION YOUR TARGET...

BLADE ARENA.

GOT MEMORIES OF THIS PLACE THAT AREN'T GOOD ONES, LOSER.

IT'S BEEN QUITE A FEW YEARS.

BUT THIS TIME --

-- YOU'RE NOT --

-- GETTING --

--AWAY!

Chapter 7

"We wanted to keep *Sigil* a science fiction series where you only *kind of* knew what to expect, because it's subject to intrusion by other forces in the CrossGen Universe."

— *Barbara Kesel*

Spaceships and Ray Guns and Aliens, OH, MY!

For writer Barbara Kesel, her first night brainstorming for her new CrossGen assignment, *Sigil*, was a Blockbuster night.

"When I knew I was working on *Sigil*, I went and re-watched every science fiction film ever done to get a sense for how science fiction up to this point had been visually represented," Barbara said. "I desperately wanted to make *Sigil* as distinctively different from the other science fiction comic books done before as possible. We knew we wanted a classic space opera adventure series, which meant that certain givens were involved – spaceships, ray blasters, aliens – but we also wanted to have our own identity, which led us to revisit those conventions with our own twists.

"So our spaceships (well, the human ones) carry 'keyhole probes' to zoom through space and their pilots lust after the newer (and easier!) technology the Saurians have developed. Our evil Saurian villians turn out to have their own noble culture and may even be smarter than the humans, and the series is generously layered with the politics of human ambition so even the good guys do bad things…for the right reasons."

Even the alien race at war with the humans had to have a twist, one hinted at in early issues but not fully revealed until later: a taste for human flesh which is literally changing their form.

"We decided that the Saurians would have the advantage over the humans ('cause everybody likes the underdog!), so the Saurian race has plasma technology and plasma-slinging bladecasters, while the humans had to come from behind with weapons that were one level more primitive. And it turns out that the Saurians have a genetic

twist that lets them be everything the humans are…except more feral."

Even the alien race at war with the humans had to have a twist. From Barbara's own notes made in 1999 during the development of *Sigil*, here is the very first written description of the Saurians:

"THE SAURIANS: Start with a vaguely raptor-like form but change

---

"When I knew I was working on *Sigil*, I went and re-watched every science fiction film ever done to get a sense for how science fiction up to this point had been visually represented. I desperately wanted to make *Sigil* as distinctively different from the other science fiction comic books done before as possible."

---

the eyes to be more alien, an optical field with a pair of pupils. Their heads are triangular, like ¾ of a Phillips-head screwdriver as the armature under a dinosaur's skin. (No room for a braincase as we know it; they have three stacked brains running down their heads and thick muscular necks.) Three colorful gill slashes line the neck; these puff with bright color when the 'saur' is angry. The bottom of the three is the poison sac. They rub darts on the secretions from this gillsac. The toxin is fatal to most other species. They have two symmetrical tactical limbs capable of holding tools and small weapons, and two working limbs that supply propulsion and strength

(Imagine a dino holding a sword in one foot while 'standing' on the other and his tail.) They are superb fighters; that extra lower limb gives them an incredible up-close advantage. They do not wear clothing as humans do, but they do decorate themselves with bands on their tactical limbs and power limbs. These bands are made of the skins of other species and decorated with metal and jewels. They wear electronic voiceboxes to emulate human speech. Their own is a series of grunts, clicks, and whistles."

The initial Saurian designs called for a drastically difference race. During development, it was determined that a more "human"-looking Saurian race fit better into the evolving mythos of the human-Saurian war because, "we needed our villains to be able to *emote*."

The whole *Sigil* universe is blindsided by the appearance of Sam and his sigil-based power. And that's where the classic concepts of science fiction get to struggle with the basic rules of the CrossGen Universe. The power of the sigil strongly impacts the human race, the Saurian race and the war between them.

"We wanted to keep *Sigil* a science fiction series where you only *kind of* knew what to expect, because it's subject to intrusion by other forces in the CrossGen Universe," Barbara said. "This is a story that co-exists with the world of *The First* and other Sigil-Bearers and sidekicks and more powerful beings who, seen from Sam's point of view, are all just impediments to exterminating the Saurians. Sam is the lightning rod for all of these different forces coming into play, intermixing their world of demi-gods and intrigue with Sam's science-fictiony world."

Sounds like a party.

I'LL JUST WAIT FOR THE BODY TO COOL TO COUNT YOUR MENTOR ON MY LIST, TCHLUSARUD--

--YOU LIZARDS ARE WICKED TOUGH TO KILL.

HREEEEEE

DO WE JOIN?

NO! CAUSE NO SHAME!

OUR LAST ORDER WAS TO HOLD!

BUT I GOT A LITTLE BIO UPDATE FOR YOUR SAM REY FILE--

--SO AM I!

YOU CAN TOSS WHATEVER KINDA ATTACK YOU LIKE AT ME!

I CAN FIX ANY DAMAGE FASTER'N YOU CAN FLING IT!

TCHARUN: SUMMER PALACE, SKYPORT.

I DON'T FEEL RIGHT ABOUT THIS.

WHAT DO YOU MEAN?

I CAN'T STAND JUST WAITING FOR SAM TO COME BACK, JeMERIK!

THIS SHIP HAS ENOUGH SPECIALIZED TECH, IT'S GOT TO HAVE A CACHE OF PERSONAL ARMAMENTS.

IF WE CAN FIND SOME WEAPONRY, WE CAN MAKE SURE SAM GETS AWAY SAFELY.

YOU'RE RIGHT, ZANNI. IT *HAS* TO HAVE WEAPONS...

...LIKE THESE?

I THOUGHT I LOOKED THERE...

YOU JUST DIDN'T HAVE THE RIGHT TOUCH.

NOT *YOUR* TOUCH, ANYWAY. LET'S LOAD UP AND FIND SAM...

TELL YOU, LOSER-- I AM PURELY ENJOYING THIS DANCE...

174

...MAKES ME FEEL LIKE A KID AGAIN!

HRAEENK

THE FORMS, TCHUSARUD.

REMEMBER THE FORMS...

WEAPONSMASTER!

YES, TEACHER. I PRAISE KHYALHTUA YOU LIVE.

THE FORMS... FOCUS...

PATIENCE!

CONTROL.

OKAY, NOW, NO COACHING--

YOU SAURS JUST WON'T DIE EASY, WILLYA?

WHAT SAY I UP THE ANTE?

177

BEING INJURED...ONLY BRINGS ME DOWN TO YOUR LEVEL... HUMAN!

AAAH!

WHACK

TCHLUSARUD! CLAIM ADVANTAGE! END THIS!

NNG!

A CHOICE, SAMANDAHL REY! LAY DOWN YOUR NECK TO ME OR WATCH ZANNIATI DIE!

THINK, LOSER.

YOU CAME CHASIN' ME, LOOKIN' FOR A WEAPON...

→GHAUUURK!←

THANK YOU, SAMANDAHL REY.

THANK ME AFTER WE'RE OUTTA HERE!

AN' CALL ME SAM.

WHY'D YOU TWO GET IN THE WAY?

I HAD IT ALL UNDER CONTROL UNTIL YOU...

I HAD HIM!

I'M SORRY... SAM. IT'S MY FAULT.

C'MON!

YOU'LL GET ANOTHER SHOT AT LOSER, SAM...

...I GUARANTEE IT!

I HAD ALL THE SHOT I NEEDED!

NOW I GOTTA GET YOU TWO SOMEPLACE SAFE...

I AM SO SORRY.

IT SLIPPED MY MIND THAT YOU'RE A *GOD* NOW!

DON'T BE ANGRY, ZANNI.

IT'S JUST--

--YOU KNOW HOW IT IS WITH ME AN' THAT SAURIAN...

...THERE'S A LOT OF GHOSTS IN THAT ARENA.

THEN FORGIVE ME FOR INTRUDING ON THEIR REST.

AND, SAM? WHERE'S THE CRASH SEATS? HOW DO WE STRAP IN?

NO NEED!

WE'RE ALREADY IN SPACE? WHEN DID THE SAURIANS GET THIS KIND OF TECHNOLOGY?

AND WHERE'S ROIYA?

THEY DIDN'T. IT'S NOT SAURIAN. THIS SHIP'S A LITTLE PRESENT FROM HEAVEN.

HEY, ROI, YOU STILL HANGIN' IN THERE?

WE'RE ON OUR WAY.

GET A MEDICIAN IN HERE NOW!

AND GET ME A COMMLINK TO THE ORBITOWER!

CONTROL, TCHLUSARUD. WE ARE NOT ANIMALS.

HI, SAM.

YOU KICK LOSER'S BUTT?

ROIYA!

WHA--?

NOT SO COMPLETELY AS I'D LIKE. HAD A LITTLE INTERRUPTION...

181

SPEW THE FORMS! I NO LONGER NEED MY REVENGE IN PERSON. I JUST WANT HIM DEAD AND HIS SHIP DESTROYED!

PLEASE BE SPARE SUITS... YES!

SHAPELESS, OVERSIZED, BAD COLOR... ...BUT *ANYTHING* WOULD FEEL MORE... *NORMAL.*

LESS LIKE A TOY.

SAFER. MORE ARMOR THAN FLUFF. OH!

Hmmm. ARMOR IT IS!

HEY-- uh... ...WHERE'D YOU GET *THAT?*

THE SHIP MADE IT FOR ME.

182

IF YOU CAN, DO IT NOW.

THEY'RE POWERING UP THE TWO-STAGE CANNON TO FRY ME...

...THE WORST PART IS HEARING THE ORDERS BEING GIVEN.

OH, SAM, SORRY IT DIDN'T--

NO, RO! NO GOODBYES!

I'M HELPIN' THE SHIP'S FIELDS WITH MY POWER--

-- WE'LL MAKE IT!

GIVE ME THAT!

WHAT D'YOU THINK YOU'RE DOIN'?

YOU USE YOUR POWER, SAM.

I'LL FLY.

I CAN MAKE THIS SHIP DO THINGS YOU'D NEVER DREAM OF...

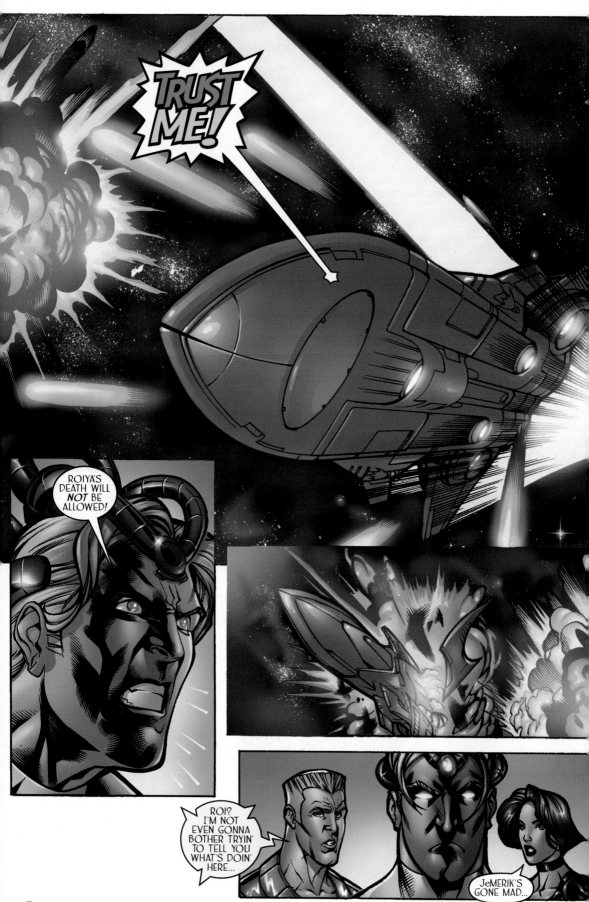

"...AND I..."

"...DON'T LIKE..."

"...HOW IT FEELS!"

189

"MORPH BOTH SHIPS INTO ONE...

"ROIYA?"

SHE HAD TO HAVE MADE IT! ROIYA'S A SURVIVOR!

ROI--?

GRAWWRRR

YOU'RE NOT QUITE WHAT I HAD IN MIND...

...BUT IT'S GOOD TO SEE YOU TOO, YOU LITTLE MONSTER.

SLOOORP

HEY!

WHO'RE YOU CALLING MONSTER?

I THINK I LOOK BETTER THAN THAT.

QUITE THE WILD RIDE, COWBOY!

WHERE TO NEXT?